Taking a Dive

Michele Martin Bossley

James Lorimer & Company, Publishers
Toronto, 1997

James Lorimer & Company Ltd. acknowledges the support of the Department of Canadian Heritage and the Ontario Arts Council in the development of writing and publishing in Canada. We acknowledge the support of the Canada Council for the Arts for our publishing program.

Cover illustration: Ian Watts

Canadian Cataloguing in Publication Data
Bossley, Michele Martin
    Taking a dive
(Sports stories)
ISBN 1-55028-573-4 (bound) ISBN 1-55028-572-6 (pbk.)
I. Title. II. Series: Sports stories (Toronto, Ont.).
PS8553.07394T34   1997   jC813'.54   C97-930949-2
PZ7.B67Ta 1997

James Lorimer & Company Ltd., Publishers
35 Britain Street
Toronto, Ontario
M5A 1R7

Printed and bound in Canada

oct stories

3055 ❧

Contents

1

Trying to Fly

"Josie, KICK!" Dale yelled.

I heard my coach's voice through the water rushing in my ears. I powered the muscles in my legs with as much force as I could and kicked explosively. But as I reached the edge of the pool and tugged off my goggles, I saw the clock and knew I hadn't done it. My time was still slow. Too slow. I hung on to the slippery tiles at the edge and looked up at Dale.

He scrubbed a hand through his short, sandy-red hair and knelt down so I could hear him over the splashing of the other swimmers. "I don't know, Josie," he said. "That 200-metre butterfly is just not coming. You're not getting the speed the way you used to. Your stroke looks choppy, not smooth and easy."

I glanced down at my hands. "Sorry, Dale. I'm really trying."

Dale frowned, looking puzzled. "I know. It should be getting easier for you by now." He lifted his shoulders in resignation. "It must just be a slump. We'll work through it. Try a few more 200-metre sets on your own, then join the team for the rest of the workout."

"Okay." I stretched my shoulders, wincing at the taut soreness. I'd worked so hard on the butterfly sprints that my muscles felt like knotted rope beneath the skin. I gave my arms a last shake and fastened my eyes on the clock. This time I would swim faster. I knew it.

But I didn't. I tried and I tried, but no matter what I did, I couldn't match my record time for butterfly. I hauled myself out of the water, perched dejectedly on the side of the pool and heaved a long, slow sigh.

What could be going wrong? Was it my kick? My stroke technique? I looked around the pool, as if I could find the answer written on the walls. Instead I saw the same old things — the lifejackets hanging on hooks against the cream-coloured concrete walls, the pull buoys and kick boards piled in big plastic bins, the orange-seated bleachers partly filled with parents who were either reading, watching the swim practice or working on laptop computers. I spent half my life in this pool, and usually the familiar scene was comforting. I sighed again and slid into the water.

In the two months since I broke the provincial record for 200-metre butterfly in my age category at our invitational competition, I had never yet come close to that time again. If I couldn't swim that race at least as fast as my record-breaker at the provincial competition, then I'd lose my chance to go on to Nationals. That was a big deal.

Swimming is my whole life. I love it. I love competing, I love practising and — since that invitational competition — I love winning. I've dreamed about becoming a top Canadian swimmer since I joined the swim team four years ago, when I was eight. I want to go to the Olympics some day ... and Worlds ... and Nationals.

Two months ago, I thought Nationals might be just around the corner. I had swum the best race of my life, and the exhilaration lasted for days. Pride and excitement bubbled inside me and I couldn't stop smiling. That is, until I got back in the pool and tried to match the time in practice and found that I couldn't.

In the next lane my friend Ross punched his hands toward the wall at the finish of a breast stroke set and popped his head out of the water to check his time. With his short-cropped brown hair and tinted goggles he looked like a bug with a brush cut.

He noticed me hanging onto the side. "What's the matter, Josie? Can't keep up with the rest of us?" he teased.

Ross has always teased me, and usually I don't mind, but lately his comments stung.

"I can keep up with anybody," I retorted, grinning. "Especially you."

"Hah. We'll see," he challenged. "Bet I can beat you in the next set."

"Bet you can't," I said hotly.

"Okay, everybody," Dale called. "Next set is arms only, eight times 100 metres of I.M. Fifteen seconds rest between each 100. Got that?"

The confident grin slipped from my face and Ross laughed. We both knew I was sunk. Ross gets all of his speed from his stocky upper body and anything involving arm and shoulder strength gives him an extra edge. I.M., or individual medley, which is a combination of butterfly, backstroke, breast stroke and freestyle, is easy for me — if I'm allowed to kick.

"Too bad, Jo," Ross scoffed. "You've lost already."

I glared at him. "Don't count your medals 'til you've won the race, Rosco."

"Get ready …" Dale kept an eye on the clock.

I snapped my goggles over my eyes and prepared to push off from the edge. Ross glanced sideways at me from the next lane and gave a mock yawn, patting his mouth with one hand, as though this race was going to require so little effort it was boring.

"GO!"

My legs jerked convulsively and I shot away from the edge like a submarine torpedo. I knew the only chance I had to outswim Ross was to make up in quickness what I lost in strength, so I swung my arms through each stroke as swiftly as possible and let my legs stream uselessly behind.

I could see Ross beside me through my now-fogged goggles and tried to push myself faster. At least the first length in I.M. is butterfly, I thought, as I gained on him. That's still my best stroke. A quiet elation filled me as I hit the turn ahead of Ross and pushed off into backstroke.

Streamline, I thought. Keep it tight. Backstroke was also a good stroke of mine. If I could just keep ahead …

I could see Ross moving up. I whipped my arms through each stroke, feeling my body jerk from the momentum.

Ross pulled beside me on the turn. The next length was breast stroke, and I gritted my teeth. It was Ross's specialty.

Sure enough, he surged forward, leaving me behind. I kept on doggedly, but I knew the race was lost. Ross and I are about equally matched in freestyle, which was the stroke in the last length, and I didn't have a chance to pull ahead.

Ross preened, standing up in the shallow end of the lane. "Told ya," he said. "I beatcha by four seconds."

I shook the water out of my ears. "No way was it four seconds," I said. "Besides, that was only one 100. There's seven more to go in this set, remember?"

Ross lost a bit of his bluster. "You want to race the whole set?"

"Scared?"

"No way!" Ross snapped his goggles back on.

"First group … five seconds," Dale shouted. "And … GO!"

In spite of my best efforts, Ross outdistanced me in every 100-metre set, although toward the end, the gap between us was narrower. I have more stamina than Ross, and he was getting tired. I tried to be a good sport about losing, but I couldn't quite squelch that last flicker of pent-up frustration.

"Too bad, Jo," he smirked as we climbed out of the pool. "You should know better than to challenge me by now."

I pressed my lips together against the irritation that swelled inside me. "You're just lucky Dale didn't give us distance sets or kicks only, or you'd have been down the toilet, and you know it."

"No way. I'm just faster, that's all."

"In your dreams," I muttered, grabbing my swim bag from the pool deck.

Ross slung his towel around his shoulders. "Josie, you shouldn't be racing against guys anyway." His eyes gleamed with mischief as he waited for me to answer.

I put my hands on my hips. "What's that supposed to mean?" I demanded angrily. I knew Ross was baiting me, but I couldn't help responding.

"Well, you know. I'm taller and stronger than you." Ross struck an exaggerated pose and flexed his small biceps. "There's not much chance you can beat me anymore. Guys are just physically ... well ..."

"Superior?" I said sarcastically.

"You said it, not me," he shrugged. "It's nothing against you, Josie, but ..."

"I'm a girl?" I finished. I felt my face grow hot and I didn't even try to control my temper. "You listen to me, Ross!" I yelled. "I can't believe you would even say such a stupid thing. You know I can lift more weight than you can on any of the leg machines in the weight room. You know I'm a better kicker than you and I'm a better distance swimmer than you, so where do you get off telling me that you're a better swimmer than I am?"

Ross stopped my tirade. "Josie, face facts. I'm not saying I'm better, exactly."

"Then what are you saying?" I insisted.

"Oh, I don't know." The provoking grin was gone from Ross's face, and he looked impatient. He picked up his swim bag and slung his towel over it. "Just forget it. Go get changed. My mom'll be picking us up in ten minutes."

I turned on my heel and stamped off to the girls' locker room. Inside I was boiling. There are times when I wonder why I like Ross, and this was one of them.

But inside the locker room, my anger began to evaporate. Arguing with Ross was the least of my worries. He was being a moronic, idiotic, stupid, infantile jerk, and I would tell him so after I got changed. That didn't bother me much. It was that 200-metre butterfly that kept nagging at me. I sat down on a bench, feeling drained and empty. What was the matter with me, anyway? Usually I finish swim workouts feeling tired, but not depressed. Now everything seemed impossible, and I was getting tired of trying.

The problem had begun right after my record-breaker at the last competition. It was as if I had psyched myself out. The harder I tried to match my best time, the worse I got. Maybe it's true, what people say about winning being all in your mind. My mind wanted to win. It was just that my body wasn't co-operating.

I sighed again, wadded my wet bathing suit and towel into a ball and shoved it into my swim bag. Ross would be waiting by now, along with Beth Kowinski, who car-pooled with us. Both Beth and Ross were in seventh grade like me.

I wrapped my fleece jacket around my shoulders and lugged my homework-stuffed knapsack, my swim bag and some overdue library books out to the parking lot. Instantly a car horn blared.

"Josie! Over here!" Ross stuck his head out of his mother's car and motioned impatiently. I hurried over, shivering as a blast of icy March wind whipped my damp hair across my face.

"Geez, Josie. We're going to be late." Ross said. "What takes you girls so long, anyway?"

Beth, who was beside me in the back seat, nudged me and cupped a hand under her chin-length light brown hair. "We have to look bee-yew-tee-full," she teased. She twisted her freckled face into an exaggerated simper.

"Yeah, right," I snorted.

Ross glanced over his shoulder from the front seat. "Well, I've got news for you. It's not working." He cracked up.

"Very funny," Beth said.

I ignored them. "Sorry I kept you waiting, Mrs. Jacobs," I said to Ross's mother.

Mrs. Jacobs turned the ignition. "That's okay, Josie." She backed out of her parking space. "We're only a few minutes behind."

Beth was wedged between me and Griff, Ross's dog. Griff looked like a black mop with four feet, and was big enough to take up the whole back seat by himself.

"Hi, Griffer." I patted his woolly head and he strained over Beth to give me a friendly lick on the cheek.

"Griff, stay down!" Mrs. Jacobs sounded cross. "I can't see through the rear-view mirror."

Hastily I pushed Griff back, and Beth emerged from underneath him, disheveled and covered with dog hair.

"Sorry," I whispered.

"It's okay," Beth stifled a giggle. "Of course, my hair's all messed up now," she added, for Ross's benefit.

"It's an improvement," Ross said, not bothering to turn around.

Mrs. Jacobs pulled the car up to the curb in front of the school. "Everybody out! Have a good day! See you after practice tonight."

"Whose mom is picking us up after school?" Ross asked.

"Mine." Beth slammed the car door. "So don't be late!" she called after him as he bounded up the school steps.

He turned at the top step, simpered and pretended to flick back shoulder-length curls. Imagining Ross with long hair instead of his bristle-topped brush cut made me giggle in spite of myself. "I'll try to be on time," he said in a high, silly voice. "But you know, I have to get my hair done first."

"Don't bother," I said, but Beth cut me off.

"Good idea," she yelled. "It'd be an improvement."

2

My Bright Idea

Earth to Josie. Come in, Josie," Mr. P. said from the front of the classroom.

The class tittered. I grinned sheepishly.

"Sorry," I said.

"That's okay, Josie. I just figured, since we're working on the solar system, you were demonstrating what it's like to be in outer space."

The class laughed, and I joined in ruefully. Mr. Panagopoulos, or Mr. P. as everyone calls him, is my nicest teacher. When he makes jokes like that, I know he's not mad, he's just trying to keep me from daydreaming. He knows how hard science was for me at the beginning of the year, but with his help I had improved my marks. I just have to pay attention. Every single minute.

But today that was practically impossible. I kept thinking about swim practice this morning, and how terrible it was. Why couldn't I swim faster? It made me so mad to think about it that I wanted to dive back in the pool and swim until I could get it right, even if it took days.

The picture in my mind made me smile. I imagined camping out at the pool, sitting on a sleeping bag, roasting a hot dog over a portable barbeque in between workout sets. Well, if that's what it took to swim that 200-metre butterfly properly, I'd do it!

My smile faded and I shook my head in frustration. Every time I tried to think of what I might be doing wrong, a little voice inside my head kept repeating, "I have to go faster. I have to go faster." The only way to go faster, as far as I could see, was to work harder.

Maybe I'd go to practice early this afternoon, I planned. Maybe I could do some extra work with the weight equipment or something, and that might help. I couldn't stop worrying. The provincial meet was only six weeks away. To qualify for Nationals, I had to swim faster than my record time. Not a lot faster, but if I couldn't even equal it now …

"Josie," Mr P. whispered, as he handed me a sheaf of the worksheets he was passing out. "Is everything okay?"

I gave him a lop-sided grimace and nodded.

"Sure?"

"Yeah," I whispered.

"Okay." He patted my shoulder and moved on to the desk behind me. A few minutes later, I felt a poke between my shoulder blades.

"Hey! What's going on?" Delaney hissed, leaning forward.

Delaney Peters is my best friend, and she sits behind me in science class. I turned to face her. Her recently cut dark hair slid over one brown eye, and she raked it back with her fingers, muttering, "I'm never cutting my hair again. Ponytails are easier." She turned her attention back to me. "So what's the matter?"

I shifted in my seat. "Same thing," I said under my breath. "I'm never going to match my time for butterfly at this rate."

"Yes, you will," Delaney said, understanding immediately. I'd been complaining about the problem to Delaney after almost every awful practice. "You're just worrying about it too much. If you'd just relax, everything would be easy."

"Yeah, right," I muttered.

Mr. P. fixed us with an exasperated glare. I turned around and began reading the question on the worksheets. I managed to answer three before my thoughts began wandering again.

"Aw, Mr. P.! You know the girls are lousy at science. Why can't we make our own groups?"

I snapped to attention.

It was Jimmy Brader who was complaining, one of the most obnoxious guys in our grade, and it took me a few minutes to understand what the discussion was about. They were talking about the lab teams that Mr. P. had assigned, and Jimmy obviously objected to being put with two girls. Jimmy was one of those big, beefy types, the kind who looked as though their muscle and fat were mixed together to form a new kind of thick body tissue. He had blunt features, and blond hair that looked like a nest of straw perched on his head. Jimmy is such a neanderthal that he once challenged me to a burping contest in fifth grade. I won, but that's another story altogether.

"No, Jimmy," Mr. P. said. "I wasn't aware that the girls are lousy at science, as you put it. Why don't you explain?"

"Boys are smarter in math and science than girls," he said. "I don't want to have to do all the work."

I sputtered with indignation. This was the second time today some male ignoramus had put down women, and I was getting touchy about it.

Jimmy heard me. "It's true," he declared loudly. "Girls just aren't very good at that kind of stuff."

I couldn't control my irritation any longer. "Is that right?" I flashed. "I'm sure Madame Curie would have been interested to hear that."

"What does some French teacher have to do with this?" Jimmy demanded. The laughter of the class caught him off guard.

"Madame Curie," I said cuttingly, "was a very famous female scientist. I'm surprised you don't know that, since you're so much better in science than I am."

Jimmy's broad face turned red. At least he has the grace to blush, I thought.

"Yeah, Jimmy," some of the girls chorused.

Jimmy brushed off the taunts easily. "I'm talking generally. Guys just have certain attitudes that help them do better in those areas."

"I think you mean aptitudes," Mr. P. put in. He was listening to the discussion with an amused expression on his face.

"Yeah, that," Jimmy said. "I read all about it in the newspaper with my dad."

"Did you read it yourself, or did your dad sound out the hard words for you?" I muttered under my breath.

Jimmy glared at me, and I heard Delaney giggle.

"Listen Josie, you can't fight facts," he said.

Mr. P. shifted in his chair. "Since you know the facts, Jimmy —" was that a touch of sarcasm in his voice? "— why don't you explain them to us?"

"Well, you know," Jimmy began. "It has to do with logic and stuff, and which side of your brain you use the most. Guys use the half that controls logic and math and science and all that stuff."

"I suppose that would make them half-wits," I said out loud. Mr. P.'s eyes twinkled in amusement.

"Oh, you're a riot, Waterson," Jimmy said. "A regular laugh factory. I'm trying to have a serious discussion here, okay?" He turned back to the class. "I just mean that there are some pretty obvious differences between how guys and girls do things. Guys are into sports, for instance. Girls like to mess around with make-up and stuff."

I actually groaned out loud. "You're kidding, right?"

"No." Jimmy's words were laced with conviction. "My sister and her friends spend hours in front of the mirror. It's like their hobby or something. They hate sports and they're crummy at math and science."

I snorted in disgust. "Since when is your sister the only example of what girls like and don't like? And since when does being a guy automatically qualify you as a great athlete? There are lots of guys who don't even like sports. And there are lots of girl athletes who are just as capable as boys."

"Oh keep dreaming, Waterson," Jimmy laughed. "No way."

"Really?" Mr. P. mused. "So you don't think that boys and girls could compete on mixed athletic teams, for instance?"

"No way," Jimmy repeated. "It's a waste of time. Guys should compete against guys. It's more fair that way. Girls just aren't as good."

The girls in the class began to mutter among themselves indignantly.

"How can you say that!" I burst out. "There are tons of women athletes that are top-ranked. How can you put them down?"

Jimmy made a stopping gesture with his hand. "Hey, hey. Calm down. I'm not saying anything against girl athletes. I'm just saying they're not as good as men."

"Why not?" I demanded.

"Look, Josie. The best male athlete will always beat the best female. He's stronger and faster. You've got to know that."

Most of the boys in class nodded in reluctant agreement.

"It depends on what the sport is," I said. "There's such a thing as brains, you know. Strategy … determination. Not everything depends on strength."

Jimmy looked doubtful.

"It's true, Jimmy. Teamwork, technique, attitude —" I looked pointedly at him "— those things all count, too. And you can't tell me that just because you're a guy you're any better at those things than I am."

Jimmy rolled his eyes. "Sure, Josie," he said.

His condescension bugged me. "Besides, we're not talking about the best against the best," I said, my voice rising. "You're saying generally boys are better athletes than girls, and I don't think that's true."

"Josie's right," Delaney said.

Mr. P. held up his hand. "Okay, everyone, I think maybe we should get back to science here." He checked his watch. "Class is almost over."

"Wait, Mr. P.," I persisted. "You don't think girls can't be good athletes, do you? Or that they're lousy at math and science?"

"No, Josie. If there's one thing I've learned in my teaching career, it's that you should never underestimate anyone, male or female."

Jimmy didn't seem impressed by this wisdom.

"Okay, then." I found myself groping frantically for some way to prove that Jimmy was wrong, and with a flash of inspiration I remembered the Athletic Day posters I'd seen plastered across the bulletin boards in the hall. "Everyone's probably heard about the school Athletic Day coming up in a few weeks, right?"

Most of the kids nodded. Jimmy looked bored.

"So," I turned to the class, "how many of you girls would be willing to compete against the boys this year and kick Jimmy's butt?"

Every girl in the class raised her hand.

"Oh, come on, Josie," Jimmy said in disgust. "Get real."

Mr. P. tried hard to keep a grin off his face, "I'll volunteer to be a coach for all the teams, if you girls will excuse the fact that I'm a member of the ... ahem, enemy."

"That's great," I said. "I'm going to talk to Mr. Wentworth right away. If he says it's okay, then we can start setting up teams."

Jimmy shook his head in disbelief. "I can't believe you're serious."

I settled into my seat, a satisfied smile on my face. "Jimmy, you're going to regret the day you ever opened your mouth."

3

A Visit with Mr. Wentworth

Delaney paced nervously up and down the hall in front of the office and checked her watch for what seemed like the fiftieth time. We were waiting for Mr. P. who had insisted on coming with us to talk to Mr. Wentworth. Mr. Wentworth was the vice-principal, and he was the one in charge of school events like Athletic Day.

My palms began to sweat. Mr. Wentworth regarded me with the same mistrust that a person would have for a crazed lunatic armed with water balloons. His opinion was based on the disaster I had created at the science fair earlier in the year. I was glad that Mr. P. wanted to help me persuade Mr. Wentworth that my idea was a good one. Otherwise I wasn't sure that Mr. Wentworth would even listen to me.

"I can't believe you said that stuff to Jimmy Brader!" Delaney said suddenly, halting in mid-stride. She shook her head in disbelief.

"Why not?" I asked, looking at the clock hanging on the office wall. Five minutes had passed. "He deserved it."

"Yeah, but now Mr. P. thinks the Athletic Challenge is a great idea. What if we lose? It would be totally embarrassing."

"What makes you think we're going to lose?" I asked evenly. "We have just as much talent as the boys."

Delaney looked exasperated. "I know that. But the boys have been training in track and field for the last month in gym class. We've been doing aerobics, remember? They've got an edge right there."

I looked up. "I never thought about that."

"And even though Jimmy is basically a gorilla-brain, he can run faster and throw harder than any of us. Gym is his best subject."

"I had kind of guessed that already," I said. I cupped my chin in my hand. "So are you saying that this was another one of my dumb ideas?"

Delaney surprised me with her vehemence. "No! It was a great idea. Guys like Jimmy have to learn that they don't own the world. My mother says, and I quote," Delaney assumed a pinched, intellectual voice, "'only the narrow-minded ascribe to preconceived stereotypes, including those of race, gender or class.'"

I blinked. "What does that mean?"

"That you shouldn't judge a person because of what they look like or where they're from."

"Oh."

Delaney's mother was a sociology professor at the university. Half the time I couldn't understand a word she said, but she was usually right.

"Sorry, girls!" Mr. P. came dashing up. He straightened his tie. "I had to meet with some students who needed extra help." He brushed at some spots that the formaldehyde had left on his sleeve and grimaced. "Frog dissection."

"Eeuuw!" Delaney wrinkled her nose.

"Come on, let's go." I was eager to get this over with, partly because I was nervous, partly because I was already late for swim practice.

We went into the office. It smelled like stacks of fresh paper, ink, and dust, a combination that always made me feel uncomfortably subdued. If strictness and discipline had an odour, I think it would smell like that.

The secretary was clicking at high speed on the computer keyboard. "Mr. Wentworth is waiting for you," she said, glancing from underneath her steel-rimmed glasses.

Mr. P. nodded, strode forward and knocked briskly on Mr. Wentworth's door. Then he pushed it open confidently and motioned for us to follow.

I swallowed and rubbed my palms against the seat of my jeans. Mr. Wentworth stood up. His balding head gleamed under the fluorescent light and I noticed that the little office was cluttered with books, files and photocopies that were stacked everywhere — the desk, the computer top, the floor, anywhere there was space.

"Hello, Josie, Delaney," he said, smiling. "Please have a seat."

Delaney and I edged past a tall stack of textbooks and sat nervously in the dusty, cracked leather visitor chairs, while Mr. P. leaned casually against a metal filing cabinet. Mr. Wentworth smoothed the front of his grey suit, sat down in his office recliner and clasped his hands forward on the desk. "Mr. Panagopoulos tells me you have something to discuss about Athletic Day," he said.

"Yes, sir," I said, trying to control the nervous quaver in my voice. "We'd like to ask your permission to hold an Athletic Day challenge. We haven't talked about all the details yet, but it would involve something like an obstacle course, and maybe some other events, like shot put or high jump."

"And a sports quiz game," Delaney added.

Sports quiz game? Since when? I raised my eyebrows questioningly at Delaney.

"Trust me," she mouthed silently.

Mr. Wentworth leaned forward. "That sounds like a splendid idea, girls. I'm sure the students would enjoy that very much."

Mr. P. held up his hand. "Wait a minute, Bob. They haven't told you everything yet."

Mr. Wentworth waited.

I took a breath. "We hoped for this one event, maybe we could have separate teams, instead of mixed."

Mr. Wentworth looked puzzled. "I don't follow you."

"You know, have teams with just girls and teams with just boys," I explained.

"Oh, well, that seems easy enough." Mr. Wentworth smiled. "You know I've always been in favour of girls and boys competing within their ranks. The gym teachers had to hound me for a couple of years before I would even consent to mixed teams."

I gulped. "No, Mr. Wentworth, you don't understand. We don't want to compete against other girls. We want to compete against the boys."

The smile vanished from Mr. Wentworth's face. "Against the boys?" he repeated.

"Yes, sir."

He leaned back in his chair. "Why?"

I looked helplessly at Mr. P.

"Go ahead and tell the whole story," he encouraged.

"Well," I said. Suddenly the whole thing seemed too complicated to explain. "I guess ... some of the guys in our class don't think that the girls can compete on the same level as boys. They think that boys are automatically better athletes than girls."

"They're stereotyping us," Delaney added. I recognized the word as one that Delaney's mother used a lot. But I saw Mr. Wentworth wince.

"I see," he said. He shot Mr. P. a glaring look. "Listen, girls, perhaps an athletic challenge is not such a good idea."

"But you just said it was a splendid idea," I protested.

"Yes …" Mr. Wentworth said slowly. "But, Josie, this isn't a matter of a fun extracurricular activity that you're asking for. You're trying to segregate the teams based on gender, and I can't allow that."

Delaney spoke up. "Excuse me, Mr. Wentworth, but we're not trying to segregate anyone. The boys and girls are already divided because of this ridiculous opinion that the boys have about athletics. If anything, we're trying to unite the students by proving that we are all on an equal footing."

I recognized more phrases from Delaney's mother in that speech. I cheered silently as Mr. Wentworth flinched.

Mr. P. jumped in. "Look, Bob, aren't you painting it a bit strong? The girls just want a chance to show the boys that they can compete with them. Athletic Day is supposed to be fun."

"Exactly. And we're turning it into an equal rights rally," said Mr. Wentworth.

"Oh, I don't think so," Mr. P. said easily.

Mr. Wentworth harumphed. "Well, I have some grave concerns regarding this idea," he said, speaking to Mr. P. and ignoring Delaney and me. "I just don't think it's fair to subject the girls to this kind of competition. It's surely going to result in a loss of self-esteem. Misguided though it might sound, I think it's best if the girls compete on their own, or with mixed teams. I don't want to see them lose confidence in themselves."

"Why would we lose confidence in ourselves?" I asked steadily.

Mr. Wentworth glanced at me and tried to soften his voice. "Because, Josie, it's quite impossible for you to compete against the boys and not feel at a disadvantage."

"I don't understand," I said slowly.

"Josie, I understand you wanting to prove yourself." Mr. Wentworth leaned forward. "I've heard that you're a tremendous athlete in the pool. I don't want any of that ambition tampered with."

"Why should it be?" I asked.

Mr. Wentworth sighed. "You're not making this easy for me to say, Josie. I just think we should leave well enough alone, that's all. Let the boys show off amongst themselves."

"What I think Mr. Wentworth is trying to say," Mr. P. said, "is that the girls should not compete against the boys, because the girls would lose."

I felt my face flame. "Is that what you think?" I asked.

Mr. Wentworth shot a look of disapproval at Mr. P. "In essence … yes."

"Why?"

"Boys simply have the upper hand in this kind of thing, Josie. It's not that I don't encourage rivalry between boys and girls. In fact, I think it's quite healthy to promote equality. But I don't want all that hard effort erased by some silly competition."

Mr. Wentworth had been speaking to me, but he finished up by looking at Mr. P.

"My mom says that true equality is based on the ability to win or lose with dignity. Babying the girls into equality is just another form of sexism," Delaney quoted.

Mr. Wentworth sighed, looking exasperated. He stared off into space for a minute, then redirected his gaze at us. "I suppose I've never thought of it that way."

"Please, Mr. Wentworth, let us try. It's more for fun than anything," I said.

He looked at Delaney's resolute face, and then at mine, which I knew was set in a stubborn frown.

"I'll give it some thought," he said. "That's all I'll promise you."

I nodded. It was better than nothing.

4

Josie the Fish

I looked at the clock in disbelief. My 200-metre butterfly was two and a half seconds slower than yesterday. I had been getting steadily slower in the last week. I smacked my fist against the water in frustration. "When will this end?"

Dale knelt down on the wet tiles at the edge of the pool. "Josie, you're trying too hard. Relax. You're way too tense."

"I know," I muttered. "But I can't help it."

"Look, take it easy. Swim a few laps, get into the rhythm. Remember how it felt to swim your record breaker? You said the stroke was easy. Smooth. Remember that when you swim. Try and relax."

I nodded. I wiped the steam from my goggles and plunged back into the water.

"Easy. Take it easy. Make it smooth." The words repeated themselves in my head. I tried to relax and remember why I loved to swim.

I used to revel in the speed and the feeling of the water rushing against my face. But today I couldn't capture that feeling, no matter how hard I tried. My muscles remained bunched and tired and knotted. My stroke stayed choppy and forced. Worst of all, nothing I did could correct it. I even tried singing inside my head and counting the laps I swam, two things I sometimes did when I got bored with workout sets.

The distraction only worked for a few minutes, and then the tension crept back.

I concentrated on swimming with long, easy, fluid strokes, but the hot, clenched feeling in my stomach wouldn't disappear. I found myself breathing in short gasps. I had to force the air into my lungs, force my arms to reach and pull. At the edge I gave up and pulled myself out of the water.

"Maybe if I stretch out a bit," I muttered. Dale glanced over, surprised to see me out of the pool, but he said nothing. He was watching Beth practise her freestyle stroke.

I watched. Beth sliced easily through the water. She slapped the water with her heels as she jack-knifed into a flip-turn and pushed off the edge. Dale moved slowly back down the pool deck, walking beside her as she swam. He didn't look at me again.

I sat down on the wet concrete. Beth was good. Really good. She'd even won a scholarship last year, so she could keep swimming with the club.

I wrapped my arms around my knees and shivered in my damp suit. The tightness in my stomach had spread to my chest and swelled upward, making my jaw clench. It was hard to swallow against that tightness.

"Hey, Jo! How come you're not swimming?" Beth called, her arms locked onto a kick board, her goggles perched on her forehead as a frothy wake churned behind her.

"Just stretching," I said, my face reddening, since it was obvious that I was doing nothing of the sort.

"Yeah, stretching your rear end," Ross said, swishing up behind Beth.

Beth pushed off the edge, kicking water deliberately up into Ross's face. "Maybe you should try stretching your *brain*!" she teased.

Ross made a grab for her ankle, but Beth was too fast and left him sputtering behind her. As he fought to catch up, I struggled with conflicting emotions.

I liked Beth, for Pete's sake. She was a friend. But just now, I felt a resentment so strong that I wanted to scream and shout and maybe even hit something. Beth was a great swimmer. In the last ten minutes, Dale had focused on her and ignored me. I felt ashamed, even as the thought flew through my mind. Ten minutes of Dale's time was nothing. I was being babyish and selfish and stupid. I knew that. It's just that I felt desperate against the frustration that had tightened my chest into an iron cage. The provincial meet loomed ahead of me like a terrible deadline. What if I didn't improve before then?

I toyed with the idea of getting back in the pool and finishing the workout, but I felt suddenly, inexplicably weary.

"Josie, are you okay?" Dale knelt beside me. "Why aren't you swimming?" His eyes looked concerned.

The wave of jealousy and frustration threatened to spill over into tears, but I gulped and hardened myself. Dale has never had time for quitters or slackers or any other kind of silliness. He coached swimmers who were serious and wanted to work. I wasn't going to show any weakness, and I was sure that Dale would think that crying because you were scared of losing and jealous of your teammates were not qualities a winner should have.

"I don't feel all that great," I said, which certainly wasn't a lie, even though I knew Dale would assume I was physically sick.

"Maybe you'd better hit the showers, then." Dale patted my shoulder. "Anytime Josie the Fish isn't in the pool, I know it's got to be something serious."

I managed a smile. Dale turned back to the team.

"Beth, let's see a little more stretch on that backstroke extension, okay? Ross, use your legs. This isn't an arms-only set. Okay, everyone, let's go on to the next set."

Dale's voice followed me into the locker room. I didn't bother to shower, even though I reeked of chlorine. Instead I changed into my clothes and sat on the bench, listlessly playing with the zipper on my swim bag.

I have always thought what Dale said about swimming was true — that it's ninety per cent hard work, nine per cent talent, and one per cent glory. Sometimes — no, a lot of the time — workouts are tough and monotonous. But it's part of training. If you want to be a serious swimmer, you have to do it, along with the weight training, running, push-ups and sit-ups.

It wasn't always fun. In fact, most of the time it was difficult. But even so, I had never felt like this.

I thought of Beth and a whole new fear took shape. I'd always believed, back in a tiny corner of my mind, that somehow Dale would help me work through this problem, that I would eventually break my time and everything would be okay again. But why wasn't he pushing me more?

What if Dale was losing faith in me? Suppose he thought I couldn't take the pressure … or the competition? I sighed and pulled a fleecy sweatshirt over my head, slightly comforted by the cozy warmth.

Breaking the provincial record had been a terrific, exciting, fairy-tale dream come true. But I couldn't help thinking that my life — and swimming — had been a whole lot simpler before it happened.

5

The Pantyhose Squad

Monday morning I shuffled into science class, yawning. Delaney was already in her seat.

"Guess what I heard," she whispered as I sat down. "Mr. P. said it's okay! He's going to tell the class this morning."

"What's okay?" I asked blankly.

Delaney rolled her eyes. "The Athletic Challenge, dummy."

"Oh." I stifled another yawn. Morning practice had been another disaster, and I was finding it harder and harder to get out of bed at five A.M. to go to the pool. I felt worse than tired. I was exhausted, and this news didn't do anything to cheer me up. I was feeling too dispirited to get ready for yet another competition, even if it didn't have anything to do with swimming.

"Listen, Dee, maybe we shouldn't go through with this after all. It's kind of dumb, really. No one will want to do it."

Delaney looked mysterious. "That's what you think."

"What do you mean?"

Before Delaney could answer, Mr. P. walked into the room.

"Okay everyone," he said. "Thanks to Josie and Jimmy's suggestion, we'll have all-boy and all-girl teams for a brand new Athletic Day challenge. I had a hard time convincing the vice-principal that this was a good idea, so I expect everyone to be good-natured about this. Teams will be mixed for all other events," Mr. P. shot Jimmy a sharp look, "and the athletic challenge will be the only event where it will be the girls against the boys. You may choose your own teams and captains. It's also up to you to decide how many teams enter the challenge. This is an optional event, so it's supposed to be fun and educational." Mr. P. gave Jimmy another pointed look.

"Yeah, right," Jimmy muttered.

Mr. P. fought to keep a smile off his face. "Well, Jimmy, since you were one of the founders of this challenge, I think we should nominate you as one of the captains."

"I second it," shouted Delaney.

"Sure, I'll be a captain," Jimmy said confidently. "I can get a great team together."

I snorted under my breath. Jimmy turned to glare at me, then put up his hand with a sly expression on his face.

"I nominate Josie as one of the girls' captains," he said.

"I second that, too," Delaney shouted.

I wanted to strangle her. "Are you nuts?" I hissed. "I just said I didn't think this was such a good idea."

"You have to go through with it now. Mr. P. set it all up for you. Besides, it was your idea."

Mr. P. ignored our whispered conversation. "Motion carried. I'm sure you'll do a fine job, Josie."

"Thanks," I muttered. Great. This was just what I needed. I hadn't given the whole idea much thought before I went shooting off my mouth. How was I going to find time to train a team for an athletic challenge, on top of my worries about swim practice?

"Tough luck, Josie. You've lost already," Jimmy Brader taunted.

The words stung. Where had I heard them before? Then it came to me. Ross had said that very same thing when he challenged me to race at swim practice the week before.

"Don't count on it," I said furiously. I wanted to say more, but I bit back the angry words. There was no point in yelling at Jimmy. The only thing he would understand was defeat ... and that was exactly what he would get!

***

I grabbed a piece of paper and a pen. "The first thing to do is to put together a list of girls who would make up a really strong team," I said. It was lunch hour. Delaney and I were huddled in the library, making plans for our team.

"Right. How about Jane Baldwin? She's almost as big as Jimmy."

I considered. "Well, maybe. She might be good at shot put and things like that, but strength and size aren't the only things that matter. Speed and agility, determination and persistence, those things are more important." I stopped myself, startled. I sounded like Dale. And for the first time, I truly realized that he was right. He always said that champions came in all shapes and sizes, and now that I was taking on a coach's position, I could see what he meant.

"For instance," I said, "Carmen Clark would be excellent."

"Carmen?" Delaney looked puzzled. "But she seems kind of ... artsy. She's definitely not a jock."

"She's a dancer. Do you know how often she trains? More than I do. She'll be in terrific shape. I guarantee it. Stacey Yee is a great gymnast. She'd be good, too. And so would Beth Kowinski, you know, from swimming?"

"Sure." Delaney chewed the end of her pencil. "What about Nancy Buko? And Leah Cameron? They're the best in our gym class in practically everything."

"Mmm-hmm. They'd be all right." I wasn't overly keen on Nancy and Leah. They were the type of girls who liked to be in charge — they were captains for a lot of the school teams and were very competitive. Still, they'd be an asset for the Challenge, especially since the goal was to win. Besides, who was I to talk? I'm competitive, too.

"How many people are on a team?"

"Eight." I tossed the paper I'd been writing on aside. "But some of the girls might want to have their own teams. I don't know ..." I was thinking of Nancy and Leah. They might not like not being in charge, and I was the captain, whether I wanted to be or not. I glanced at the clock. "It's almost time for class. And I have to go to swim practice right after school. I can ask Beth then, but how am I going to talk to everyone else about joining the team?"

"That's all right," Delaney said. "I'll ask all the girls about it after school, and then let you know, okay?"

"Okay," I answered, relieved. "Thanks a lot, Dee."

"No problem. I'll call you tonight."

***

After supper I found myself waiting for the phone to ring. Beth had told me she'd join the team, especially when she found out that Jimmy had recruited Ross, but I couldn't wait to find out about everyone else. I tried to concentrate on my homework, but gave up after I discovered I'd read the same page three times without remembering anything about it. I flopped down on my bed and tapped a pencil thoughtfully against my teeth. I gazed up at the swimming poster on my ceiling. I wiggled my big toe through a hole in my sock. I scratched an itchy place on my ankle. I sighed and glanced at my watch.

Seven o'clock. I jumped up, unable to stand the suspense anymore. Delaney should be calling any minute, but I couldn't wait any longer. I dialed her number.

"Dee?" I said when she answered. "What's going on?"

"Well, there's good news and bad news," she said. "Which do you want first?"

I grimaced. "The good news."

"We have Carmen and Jane, like you wanted. Right now we also have Leah, but I don't think she'll be staying long."

"Why not?"

"That's part of the bad news. Nancy started her own team, and I think Leah will probably want to be on hers, even though I asked her first and she said she'd join us. Nancy also asked Stacey first and has most of the girls who are decent in gym on her team already."

"So who do we have for the last two places on our team?"

"Randi Sloski and Marion Elbridge."

"Randi and Marion?" I could barely keep the horror out of my voice. Randi was known around school as a super-klutz. If there was a paint bucket anywhere near, she'd step in it. If there was water on the floor, she'd slip on it. She was a disaster magnet.

Marion was one of the smartest kids in school, and she was a terrific actress. She'd won the lead in the school play last fall, even though they had planned to give it to a ninth grader. The only problem was, she had no athletic talent. Zero. Zip.

Marion wasn't one of those girls who are afraid to get dirty or break a nail or anything. She just wasn't very good — no, she was terrible — at sports.

"Oh, no!" I moaned. What had I gotten myself into?

"Sorry, Josie. But what could I say? They both asked to join, and I wasn't about to be a jerk and say no, that we only wanted good athletes."

"I know."

"Besides, there's hardly anybody left to have. That's what I was going to tell you in class today, before Mr. P. talked to everybody. All the girls want to get in on it. You wouldn't believe some of the stuff Jimmy and his friends have been saying."

"Like what?"

"Oh, they're bugging us, saying things like we're the pantyhose squad and stuff."

"The pantyhose squad!" I bristled.

"They're just being dumb. But a lot of the girls are getting ticked off, so just about everybody has joined a team."

"Oh." This wasn't quite what I had envisioned. Somehow I had figured my team would be the only team.

"So, that's good, really. It shows how terrific your idea is. Plus, it'll be more fun this way."

"Yeah, but I wanted to be the one to kick Jimmy's butt," I said. "Now we haven't got a chance."

"Sure we do. And we can still show him that girls are good athletes. Wasn't that the point in the first place?"

I tried to remember. "Yeah. I guess so."

"So, what difference does it make who beats him? I know it will be more embarrassing if we don't, but with all the girls trying, at least one team has got to win," Delaney pointed out.

"Yeah," I said dismally. "But with Randi and Marion, it sure won't be us."

6

A New Strategy

Okay, everyone," I called above the excited chattering that echoed in the corner of the empty gym. "Hey, you guys … come on …" No one was paying the least bit of attention. I glanced at my watch. Mr. P. was supposed to meet us for our first after-school team practice, and he was late. There was only half an hour left before I had to be at the pool, and someone had to take charge. "HEY! LISTEN UP!" I hollered.

The noise ceased, and the girls all stared at me.

"Sorry," I said. "But we have practically zero time to get ready for this. The boys have been practising track and field events for a month in gym class, so we have a lot of catching up to do."

Leah looked scornful. "We'll never catch up, not with this bunch."

I swallowed. "I know it's not going to be easy, but we want to try and at least make a good showing."

"A good showing?" Leah asked. "Josie, I joined this team because I heard you wanted to win. If you don't want to win, then I'm out of here."

"Of course I want to win," I retorted. "But the truth is, we're at a disadvantage here."

"That's for sure." Leah looked pointedly at Marion and Randi.

"That's not what I meant." I was losing patience. "Look, we have no time for lousy attitudes. So either put a cork in it and work with us, or take a hike, okay?"

I felt stunned. I've never sounded so bossy in my life. In fact, I sounded just like my coach, Dale. And it worked.

Leah muttered under her breath. "Nancy's team is full, so I guess I'm staying," she said sullenly.

I felt a rush of victory. "Good. Now let's get to work."

***

But later, in my bedroom, I groaned to myself. Mr. P. had given out a sheet explaining the events in the Athletic Challenge. There was a 100-metre sprint, shot put, and an obstacle course involving stepping through tires, weaving in and out of pylons, and swinging over mats on the climbing rope to pick up an object, then racing back through everything to the finish line. There were sit-up and push-up competitions, rope climbing, hurdles, and, of course, the sports quiz.

We spent much of the team meeting trying out our skills on each event. But we were all hopeless. As Leah said at the end of practice, "We're all a bunch of bumbling bunglebutts." That pretty much said it all.

None of us knew the answers to any of the sports trivia questions that were given as examples. Randi nearly dislocated every joint in her body trying to do the obstacle course, Marion tripped over the hurdles, and I thought Delaney was going to give herself a hernia trying to shot put.

It was a disaster.

Why did I get myself into these things, I wondered, as I stretched out on my bed. Last fall I had entered the science fair, mostly because I got into a fight with Melissa, my super-achieving, older sister. That had turned out to be a borderline catastrophe. Now I was in another mess, mostly because I'd lost my temper with Jimmy Brader.

There was a tap on my door.

"Josie?" Melissa stuck her head in the room. "Mom's ordering pizza for supper. Do you want pepperoni?"

"Vegetarian." My voice was muffled by my quilt, but I didn't bother to raise my head from my face-down position on the bed.

"Jo, is there something wrong?"

Dumb question, I thought.

"Wait a minute, dumb question, right?" Melissa laughed. "Obviously something's wrong. Want to tell me what?" She leaned against the door frame and pushed her light blond hair out of her eyes. For once, her dazzling smile was missing. I could tell she was really concerned.

I considered. Until recently, Melissa had been my biggest rival, and a constant pain in the rear end. But we'd talked about things a few months ago, and I trusted her more now.

I rolled over. "Okay, here's the deal. Have you heard about the seventh-grade challenge for Athletic Day?"

"Hmmm. Nope. Ninth graders are playing field sports for Athletic Day. Why?"

"Well, it was my idea," I said. I explained the whole story and left Melissa sitting with a puzzled frown on her face.

"I see what you mean," she said slowly. "If you lose badly, Jimmy Brader will bug you about it for the rest of your life. He sounds like that type."

"I know," I agreed.

"Even if you don't beat him, and I'm not saying you can't, you have to at least show him that girls can compete on the same level."

"I know," I repeated.

"But you have a totally unco-ordinated team, and hardly any chance to improve before you compete."

"I know," I said for the third time. "So what am I going to do?"

A crafty look stole across Melissa's face. "Outsmart him."

7

Practise ... Practise ... and More Practise

O kay, listen up," I announced at the team meeting after school in the gym. I faced the girls, who were sitting cross-legged on the floor and this time everyone quieted down immediately. I really felt like a coach.

"We have a whole new game plan," I said, my voice echoing in the empty room. "This idea is so basic, I'm surprised we never thought of it before. My sister Melissa helped me with it last night and —"

"Spare us the details and get to the point," Delaney joked.

I wrinkled my nose at her. "Okay, here it is. The guys have all been training at track and field events in gym, right? So the guys on the challenge teams have all been practising the same events. That means nobody has had any specialized training."

"So?" Leah said.

"It means that the guys probably haven't thought too much about who is going to do each event. They're probably just going to pick the events they like best, or think they're good at."

"What's wrong with that?" Leah said.

"Nothing, unless you're going up against a team who has done some specialized training. And that's us."

"I still don't get it," Leah complained.

"Well …" I floundered for a minute, then thought of what Dale might say. "I've assigned an event to each of us, based on our individual strengths. And we'll each practise that one event only and get really good at it, instead of wasting time practising all the events."

"And being lousy at all of them," Delaney finished.

"Uh … well, yeah," I said. "So, Leah, because you're our best runner, you'll do the 100-metre sprint, okay?"

Leah looked pleased. "Sure." She leaned back on her hands and her face lost the belligerent look I'd grown used to. I was glad Leah seemed happy, because with her long legs, sturdy build and no-nonsense attitude, she was one of the best athletes we had. She even looked the part today, dressed in a gray sweatshirt and gray cotton shorts, with her dark blond hair tied back in a short, spiky ponytail.

"Carmen, you have the most agility because of your dancing, so I put you in the obstacle course."

"Okay." Carmen's voice was soft. She pushed back the cloud of dark brown hair that framed her pale face, and her large blue eyes regarded me calmly. She looked almost too wispy and fragile to compete in an athletic contest, but I knew her appearance wasn't what it seemed. I had seen her dance before in school recitals, and Carmen was made of steel.

"Beth, you have a lot of upper arm strength from swimming, so you're doing the rope climbing competition. Jane, of course, is shot put."

Jane nodded, her thickset upper body and chunky arms giving all the explanation anyone needed.

"Marion, we put you on the sports quiz, okay? You have the best grades, and I figured you'd be good at that."

Marion laughed. "And the worst at everything else, you mean. That's okay, I like sports trivia. I'll have to start digging through all the old Sports Illustrated magazines." She smoothed her white T-shirt over her plaid flannel shorts and flipped her bouncy red-gold hair back from her shoulders.

"Okay. Delaney is doing hurdles," I said. "I'm doing push-ups, because I have to practise them all the time for swimming, so I'm used to them, and Randi is doing sit-ups. That covers everything. Anyone have any questions?"

"Why am I doing hurdles?" Delaney exclaimed. "I'll fall on my face!"

"Because you're fairly good at all track and field stuff, Dee, but you don't have a specialty. That was the only event left that I could give you."

Randi stuck up her hand. "What if you don't like the event you're doing? I kind of wanted to do the obstacle course."

"You've got to be kidding," Leah teased with a grin. "Stick to sit-ups, Randi. At least you can't trip over them."

Randi made a face. "Thanks a lot." Even though Leah was just kidding, a hurt expression settled on Randi's thin, plain-featured face. She was fine-boned and wispy like Carmen, but she was also gangly and not very strong.

"Randi, you could do the obstacle course if you want," I said quickly. "But Carmen's dance training will make it a lot easier for her. Besides, I picked you for sit-ups especially." I swallowed. What I was going to say next was sort of a lie, but a very necessary one. "I saw you doing them in gym class last week, and I'm pretty sure if you practise you could win that event for us."

Randi's face lit up. "Really?"

"Yeah."

"Okay. I'll do sit-ups, then." Randi stuck her tongue out at Leah, who rolled her eyes at me.

Before we split up into pairs to work at our events, I caught Leah by the elbow.

"Haven't you ever heard of positive attitude training?" I hissed. "You're going to wreck Randi's confidence if you don't shut up, and we don't need any more problems. So quit teasing her, okay? Especially if you want to win."

Leah looked surprised. "I was just kidding around," she said.

"Well, don't. We're a team," I said. "And we have to stick up for each other."

Leah nodded. "Yeah. Because Jimmy sure won't."

I felt relieved. I'd solved one more problem, and things were actually looking up. Jane and Leah headed out to the field to practice, Delaney and Carmen went with them to check out the obstacle course and the hurdles, Marion went to the library and Beth began stretching out in a corner of the gym. Randi and I also stayed in the gym to work on sit-ups and push-ups.

"Do you really think I could win the sit-ups event?" Randi asked shyly. "Even competing against boys?"

"I know you can," I said, crossing my fingers behind my back. "We just have to practise."

And we did. Everyone worked hard. Even Randi surpassed everyone's expectations. I had decided to give her the sit-ups event because it seemed the least likely for her to mess up, but after I had boosted her confidence, she really excelled. By the time we held our third team practice, with just two weeks left until Athletic Day, I was beginning to think that Randi wasn't klutzy at all, just overly self-conscious.

"That was terrific!" I yelled that afternoon as Randi collapsed, sweaty and gasping on the mat.

"How many did I do?" Randi croaked.

"Fifty-nine!" I said triumphantly. "Now, next time, keep the pressure on your hips. You kept flopping around, even with me holding your legs. You'll get more speed if you can stay still. Ready to try again?"

Randi looked at me and groaned.

Marion slammed the gym door behind her and came running over, her arms full of photocopies. "Look, you guys! I found tons of newspaper articles about all kinds of Olympic athletes."

"Where'd you get all that stuff?" I gaped.

"Off the microfiche in the library. Did you know that bobsledding is an Olympic sport?" Marion looked flushed with excitement. "So is some weird thing called luge. It's kind of like tobogganing."

"Tobogganing is an Olympic sport?" Randi looked confused.

"No, luge is. Never mind. The point is, there's tons of information about sports. If Mr. P. asks any hard questions, I'll be ready. We're going to completely squish Jimmy's team in this event."

"Good. At least somebody's prepared." Leah looked sour as she stomped into the gym. "I've been out there practising, and it's not doing me any good."

"What's the matter?" I asked.

"I can't get my stupid start right," she complained. "If I could just get out of the starting block quicker, I'd cut off a lot of time."

I scrambled up off the mat. "Let's see."

We went outside to the practice field through the gym's side door. Gray clouds were scudding across the sky and a cold wind cut right through my T-shirt. Shivering, I wrapped my arms around myself and shifted from one foot to the other.

Leah ignored the cold and knelt in the damp grass, placing her feet carefully in the starting block.

"Is that thing pinned down tight?" I asked.

"Of course."

"Take your marks. GO!" I yelled.

Leah pushed off and sprinted down the field, stopping after twenty metres or so.

"Well?" she asked, jogging back.

I frowned. "Do it again."

Leah obliged, but even after the second time, I still wasn't sure.

"Once more." I shook my head as Leah jogged back for the third time. "I can't see anything wrong. I'm no track expert, but your start seems good."

Leah gestured in exasperation. "What can I do then? I need to make it faster."

I thought. "My coach at the swim club told me to visualize exploding off the start. Imagine bursting with energy, right when the gun goes off."

Leah stared. "That sounds completely stupid."

I shrugged. "Try it."

"No way." Leah kicked at the metal pin that fastened the starting block to the grass. "That's not going to help."

"How do you know, unless you try?" I argued. "Being stubborn isn't going to help improve your time, you know."

She eyed me sceptically.

"Just go! But really try it. Don't just fool around."

"I feel so dumb," Leah muttered. She placed her feet carefully in the block and lowered her body into the start position. "This is a bunch of hooey-balooey."

"Feel the power," I intoned, trying not to laugh. "It's surging through your legs … your toes …"

"Josie, cut it out. Let's just do this."

"Okay. Ready? Concentrate." I watched Leah tense, an intent expression on her face. "Take your marks … GO!"

She shot away from the block like a bullet, legs and arms pumping. She skidded to a stop about twenty metres away, with an astonished grin.

"I think maybe it worked. Kind of, anyway. I felt a lot faster," she said. "Did I look any better?"

"Yeah, I think so. You looked like you came off the block a lot quicker, but I never timed you," I said.

"I never thought any of that hooey-balooey stuff worked, but maybe I was wrong." Leah pulled the stop watch from her sweatshirt pocket and tossed it to me. "I want to try it again. Can you get a time for me?"

I shook my head as I glanced at my own watch. "I have swim practice in about ten minutes, and I'm already going to be late. I'll get Delaney or Jane to come out."

Leah just nodded, already kneeling down, fixing her feet into the block. Her knees were stained green from the spring grass.

"Okay, see ya," she said.

I ran toward the gym door. The wind had raised goose-flesh on my bare arms, and the welcome warmth of the gym wrapped around me as I burst inside. I handed the stop watch to Delaney, grabbed my homework from the dusty corner where I'd left it, and raced out to the school parking lot.

Mom wasn't there yet. I hopped up and down with impatience and shoved my arms into the sleeves of my jacket.

I started thinking about how well the challenge team was shaping up. I still wasn't sure we could beat Jimmy, but it felt good to help Randi and Leah improve. Sometimes a few suggestions could really make a big difference. And then, as I was standing there in the parking lot with the cold wind swirling dust and tiny bits of gravel around my ankles, a thought hit me. Maybe all this time I hadn't been paying enough attention to Dale's suggestions. He'd corrected me — the same way I'd corrected Leah and Randi today — but I hadn't really listened. Not really. I'd just kept doing the same things over and over, hoping that eventually the hard work would pay off. Maybe if I tried the same technique — focusing on little details that only a coach could pick out — it would work for me, too. After all, Leah hadn't listened to me at first, but look at how she had improved after I had helped her. And Dale was a much better, tougher coach than I was.

I felt a mixture of relief and hope as I thought about this potential answer to my problems. As Mom's car pulled up beside me, gravel crunching under the tires, I found that I was smiling.

Sometimes inspiration hits in the oddest places.

8

Beth's Advice

Better. It's still not there, but it's better." Dale clicked the stop watch and gripped it in his fist.

I took a deep breath. Afternoon practice was almost over, and I'd been working almost non-stop on my 200 fly. "Okay. So I'm improving. What now?"

Dale stared off into space for a moment. "Your technique is good. We'll start tapering soon, and hope that the rest gives you the extra energy you need."

"Tapering? But Dale, my time's not down yet. I'm not ready to taper," I said, then blushed. It had taken less than half an hour for me to break my promise about listening to Dale. I could have shoved my fist down my throat.

"I really think tapering will make a difference, Josie. You've been working like a trouper, and the extra rest might help."

"Okay, if you think so," I said contritely. "Tapering" is the term used to describe the lighter workouts that swimmers do as they get closer to competitions. The idea is that a swimmer will achieve a high level of speed and endurance during heavy workouts, and by tapering off, that speed may possibly increase.

But the idea of tapering right now scared me. I wasn't up to maximum speed, and you should be before you taper. Did that mean that Dale thought that I wouldn't get any faster before Provincials? Did he think that my record-breaker was just one brilliant but flukey performance? I felt my shoulders tighten up.

I reminded myself to listen to Dale — that he knew better than I did what would increase my speed. But I still felt worried.

"Try a couple of 100-metre sprints. Mix up your strokes a little, then come back to fly, okay Josie?"

"Okay." I snapped my goggles over my eyes and began the sets. I concentrated on my technique and tried to relax. After the last 100, I reached up for the starting block and clambered out of the pool. I wanted to stretch out before I geared up for the 200 fly. As I shook my shoulders to loosen the muscles, I saw Beth punch her hands toward the edge in the lane next to me. She pulled off her goggles and draped her body over the lane rope, gasping for breath.

Dale was already checking her time. "Great job, Beth!" he called. His deck shoes squidged on the wet tile as he knelt down and thumped her heaving shoulders proudly. "You keep up that kind of performance, and we'll see a medal out of you at Provincials for sure! That 400-metre freestyle of yours is a winner."

I felt my heart sink down to my toes. Beth puffed and looked up at me with a grin. "Does that mean I can go home now?" she teased Dale.

"Absolutely not!" Dale tried not to laugh. "Just because you're faster than ever is no excuse for slacking off. So get back in there and do another 400."

Beth groaned good-naturedly and pulled on her goggles. As she ducked back under the water, Dale walked down the side of the pool, watching her swim with an intent expression on his face.

I bit my lip. What I had been afraid of was actually happening before my eyes. Dale had another swimmer to focus on, and I was slowly losing my place in the spotlight.

I pressed my lips into a hard line. I'd just have to fight my way back up, that's all. I dove into the water, determined to make this 200-metre butterfly the best one of all. The water rushed past my face. My arms hacked at the water with all my strength, and I kicked so hard I almost dislocated my knees. As I hit the edge I looked up at the clock.

I don't believe this, I thought. I gulped hard against the burning in my throat. My time was slow. Slower than the sets I'd swum with Dale less than half an hour ago! What was the matter with me? As I sagged against the lane rope, its plastic floats digging me in the ribs, I noticed that the pool was practically empty. Most of the swimmers had finished practising. Just good ol' Josie was left, still swimming, still getting nowhere, I thought grimly.

"Josie?" Beth said hesitantly. She was wrapped in a navy towel with the ends tucked into the shoulder straps of her swimsuit. Her dark hair was tangled from blotting it dry. "I just … I forgot my cap and goggles out here and I saw you swim. I don't want to be pushy or anything … but I know how much getting your time down for 200 fly means to you … and I think I might know what you're doing wrong."

"You do?" I stared at her in disbelief. If Dale didn't know, and I didn't know, how could Beth know?

She interpreted my look and shifted uncomfortably. "Well, maybe. I've been watching you a lot, you know. Especially today. And I saw you doing something … You don't do it every time. It's kind of weird, actually. It comes and goes."

"What is it?"

"Your arms. You do these really wide circles with your arms and you don't dig your hands down in front of your face, but more like here." She demonstrated. "It's almost like you get your arms three-quarters of the way up, then plunge them in. You're not completing the arm stroke. That's got to affect your speed."

"How come Dale didn't notice?" I asked.

She shrugged. "I don't know. Probably because you don't do it all the time. It's only really obvious once in a while. And those are always your slowest times."

I thought about what she said. "And I was doing that funny stroke when you watched me just now?"

"Yep."

A light dawned. "I was tense … worried about what Dale said about tapering. I wasn't thinking about the race." And, I thought guiltily, I was busy being jealous of you. "Every time I've swum a slow time … a really slow time, I was too tense to concentrate. I'd just think, 'Go faster. Go faster.'"

Beth nodded wisely. "You're psyching yourself out. And then you do that funny arm thing, and the whole swim goes down the tubes."

"You're right!" I shouted. "And if I fix my arms, then even when I'm tense, I should still swim okay."

"Girls, time to go!" A lifeguard stuck her head out from the pool office. "Public swim is starting."

I groaned. "Not now!"

Beth patted my arm. "Tomorrow. Try again tomorrow."

9

A Test of Time

I hesitated at the edge of the pool the next morning. The water was chilly around my toes. Did I really want to swim that 200 fly again? What if I still failed? Why couldn't I have taken up a sport that was easier, like kick-boxing or mud-wrestling? Did I really want to jump in that cold pool at five-thirty in the morning? Wouldn't I rather be at home in bed?

"Oh, go on. Wimp."

I turned. I was expecting Beth, but Ross stood behind me, holding his goggles in one hand. For once he was early to morning practice. I'd stopped car-pooling with Ross for a while, and without Beth and I picking him up, he was notorious for sleeping through his alarm clock and arriving at practice late.

I didn't know what to say. I hadn't really spoken to Ross since this whole thing with Athletic Day came up, and I was still kind of mad at him for the dumb things he had said a few weeks ago.

I searched for a retort, something that would let Ross know that I hadn't forgiven him. But before I could open my mouth, he blurted out, "Josie, I ... you know ... wanted to say I'm sorry." The tips of his ear grew red. "You know, for giving you a hard time about breaking your record and all that."

"It's okay," I said, taken by surprise. I wasn't sure if I meant what I said.

Ross sensed this and looked embarrassed. "I mean it. And I wanted to tell you, you know, about this Athletic Day thing. At first I thought you were crazy, but now … you know … Brader's being a real knob about the whole thing. He asked me to be on his team, and you wouldn't believe the stuff we're putting up with. And the guy is like … totally sure you're going to lose, just because you're a girl."

I felt my neck stiffen with anger. I jutted my jaw, and was about to tell Ross exactly what Jimmy could do with his attitude, but Ross stopped me.

"Wait. I just want to say that I think he's wrong. I bugged you before about male superiority and stuff, but Jo, I never really believed it. Not like Jimmy does."

"Thanks," I said. I didn't know what else to say. We stood there looking at each other.

Ross gravely handed me his swim bag, which weighed a ton. "So, seeing as how I'm not superior, would you mind carrying my stuff for me? I'm feeling kind of weak today."

Ross kept a straight face, but I knew he was covering the sincerity of his apology with a joke. I promptly dropped the bag on his toe.

"Yowtch!" Ross capered around, clutching his foot. He pulled an exaggerated face, and I couldn't help giggling.

"Friends?" I said.

"Well, I don't know," Ross grumbled, massaging his big toe. "I have a rule. Anyone who tries to break my foot is no friend of mine."

I grinned at him.

"So, you are going to kick Jimmy's butt, right?" Ross began to stretch his shoulders out. There were only a few minutes left before practice started.

A giggle caught in my throat and I made a strangled sound. "Well, actually …" I hesitated. "I don't know if we can beat him." It was a relief to blurt out my doubts, after hiding them for so long. "Even though Melissa helped me figure out a training plan, I'm not sure we're going to be good enough."

"Jimmy's team is good, but not that great. I should know. I'm on it."

"Yeah," I sighed. "But so is ours. Good, but not great."

"So we should be equally matched. You're not saying that the boys' "good" is better than the girls' "good," are you?"

I bristled. "No, I'm not! But geez, Ross, I'm not stupid! I got into this fight with Jimmy Brader because he thinks boys generally are better athletes than girls. I wanted to prove that he's wrong. But I also know that some of the guys are starting to have a physical edge on the girls."

"Yeah, puberty does that," Ross said, pulling a solemn face.

I whacked him on the arm. "I'm serious, you doorknob."

"Quit worrying, Jo. You know Dale says that winning isn't based just on strength. You said so yourself, about how talent, determination, strategy and everything count more."

"I know," I muttered.

"Well, then, go for it!"

"Yeah." A mental picture of Jimmy, his muscles bulging, rose up in my head. I dismissed the image. I had other things to worry about right now. Or not worry about, I corrected myself. Worrying was what had gotten me into this swimming mess to begin with.

"Hi!" Beth said breathlessly. "I tried to get here early, but Dad's car wouldn't start and he had to get Mom up to tell her we were taking her minivan."

"That's okay. I haven't done anything yet."

"What's up?" Ross asked curiously.

"Oh, nothing," Beth said, with fake coolness. "Josie just figured out what was causing her slump, that's all."

"You mean, *you* figured out what was causing my slump," I said.

Beth poked me, and Ross made an impatient gesture.

"Who cares? What's the problem?" he said

"I do an incomplete arm stroke when I get tense, and then I psych myself out and get tenser."

"More tense," Beth corrected.

"That too."

"Well, why are you wasting time yakking?" Ross demanded. "Get in there and swim. I'll time you."

Ross, having gotten his apology out of his system, was obviously back to normal.

I took a deep breath, and a tiny spurt of fear shot through me. I was afraid to face the clock again.

"Come on, Josie. Get going."

"Just wait!" I snapped, adjusting my goggles. "Give me a second, okay?"

Ross pulled a stop watch out of his swim bag. "We'll even make it official." He sat down on the edge of the pool, and clicked the watch to reset it.

"You're making me nervous. I do that thing with my arms when I'm nervous," I warned.

"You'll be more nervous at Provincials. You ready?"

"No."

"Take your marks." Ross held his thumb over the stop watch button. Beth watched silently, and the other swimmers stretching out and chatting before practice stopped to see what was going on.

Relax, I thought, feeling my shoulders tense. It's going to be okay. Relax.

The lane ropes bobbed gently in the water. I leaned forward slightly and licked my lips.

"And ... go!"

The water hit my face with a cold slap. My legs jerked, and I floundered for a second before I hit my stroke.

As I rose up from under the water to take a breath, I heard Ross yell, "Josie, concentrate!"

I sank under and began to pull through the water with smooth, even strokes. Extend your arms, I ordered myself. Pull.

For the first time in a long time, I didn't feel like I was struggling against the water. Instead, I used all my strength to push through it. My breathing felt easy — not the usual choking, sputtering feeling that I'd grown so used to in the past few weeks.

Second lap. Third lap. I'd pictured myself swimming this race a thousand times. Fifth lap. Sixth lap. My arms started to get tired, but I kept focusing on that perfect stroke. I pictured the speed, and pushed myself.

The last lap. I strained for the edge. I came up gasping. I threw off my goggles and blinked away the water running down my face.

"Well?" I demanded.

Ross looked up with maddening slowness. "You did it, kid!" He shoved the watch in my face.

Beth did a wild dance on the pool deck, shouting. "Only two-tenths of a second slower than your record! And you fumbled your dive, you weren't wearing a racing suit, and you haven't tapered down. You can cut off two-tenths, easy."

I looked at the watch and shrieked.

10

The Big Day at Last

The smell of crushed grass and new dandelions rose off the field. I turned so the glare from the sun was out of my eyes and watched the flurry of activity around me.

Kids were everywhere, stretching, talking, finding friends. Athletic Day had finally arrived. The ninth graders were dividing up into teams for soccer and softball. Some grade eight students were mixing lemonade in large jugs and hoisting them onto the cafeteria tables that were placed along the outside wall of the school. Mr. Wentworth, hardly recognizable in blue sweatpants and a white T-shirt with a whistle on a thick black string hanging around his neck, burst out from the gym doors, his arms laden with cardboard trays of doughnuts. He set them down with great care beside the lemonade and walked off to supervise the placement of the hurdles.

Two teachers were setting up high jump stations, and Mr. P. was marking off a finish line in white chalk dust on the grass for the 100-metre sprint. The carton containing the chalk jerked in his hand, and the finish line began to look like a series of white blobs.

Mr. P. ran his hand through his hair in exasperation as I walked up.

"Hi, Josie," he said. He rubbed his sneakered foot in the dust to smooth it into a wobbly line.

"Want help?" I offered.

"Sure."

I began trampling the chalk dust, spreading the blobs carefully over the grass.

"There. That'll do." Mr. P. closed the chalk container and surveyed our work. "Just as long as we can see it. It doesn't have to be a work of art." He looked at me. "So, all ready for the big event?" he asked.

"As ready as we'll ever be, I guess," I answered uncertainly.

Yesterday I'd felt ready to tackle the world. But today, I wasn't so sure. In spite of feeling like I'd triumphed over myself at swim practice, I still had to triumph over Jimmy Brader, or endure his teasing for the rest of my life.

Mr. P. handed me eight red tags. "You're the red team. Nancy is yellow, Jimmy is blue, and Phil is green."

"That's it? Only four teams are competing in the challenge? I thought the whole grade was doing this."

Mr. P. grinned. "Well, I suppose they were, until they found out how hard they'd have to work to beat the top team." He tugged meaningfully on a lock of my hair. "Go get 'em, kiddo."

I smiled weakly and grabbed Delaney as she walked by. "Dee," I hissed. "How come there aren't more teams for the challenge? I thought you said that everyone wanted to do it."

"They did. But you know ... I guess they just bailed out or something. It's not easy to get a team organized and stick with it."

"Tell me about it." I rolled my eyes. "But that means that there are only two girls' teams — us and Nancy's. The odds aren't great. What if Jimmy beats us both?"

Delaney shrugged. "Don't think about it. It might not happen."

"That's very comforting," I said sarcastically.

"Take it easy. You don't compete very well when you get yourself all tied up in knots, remember?"

I sighed. "Yeah, I remember." I'd told Delaney what had happened at swim practice the day before. I'd also told her about Beth helping me realize how I psyched myself out when I tensed up.

"TWEET!" Mr. P.'s whistle shrilled across the practice field.

"Okay, everyone, this is it!" he bellowed. "Grade sevens, line up over here with me, grade eights are in the gym, and grade nines are with Ms. DePalma at the other end of the field. You'll be divided up into groups and assigned a teacher to work with for the day. All teams will rotate through each event. Got that? Okay, let's go!"

The students scattered. Delaney and I stuck together. The grade sevens congregated in front of Mr. P.

"All right, everyone. Divide yourself into groups of eight. Each group will start at a different event. After you've completed all the events, all grade seven students will meet back on the practice field to watch the Athletic Challenge."

There were a few weak cheers.

I found myself in Mr. P.'s group, along with Delaney, Leah and ... gulp ... Jimmy Brader. What colossal bad luck!

"Hey, JoJo," he teased. "All ready?"

I nodded stiffly.

Mr. P. herded us toward the long jump pits, which were located on the perimeter of the practice field and were our first event. He rubbed his hands together enthusiastically. "Okay, guys. This is going to be fun!"

"Yeah!" Jimmy echoed, with a sly look at me. I ignored him and began stretching the backs of my legs.

"Yeah," Leah said belligerently, "it sure is." She gave Jimmy a wicked grin and some of the bluster fell from his face.

I exchanged looks with Delaney and permitted myself a small smile. Leah's forceful attitude had its merits, after all.

But that smile vanished when Jimmy, who was obviously geared to show me up, dashed to the sand pit, and with legs churning and arms windmilling, executed an excellent jump.

He jogged back to his place in line. "Not bad, eh?" he said. "Can ya beat that?"

I didn't answer. When my turn came, I ran as fast as I could toward the pit and leaped into the air with all my strength. My feet skidded out from under me as I landed, and I ended up on my rear end, covered in sand. Fortunately for me, most of the other students were busy with their own events, but my team saw the whole thing, and that was bad enough. Jimmy thought it was hilarious, and even Delaney had her hands clamped over her mouth, trying not to laugh.

"Good try, Josie," Mr. P. consoled. "Are you all right?"

"Yeah." I brushed the sand off my behind and tugged at the waist band of my gym shorts.

I hated our school's gym gear. It was an ugly shade of green trimmed with brown and it made me feel like an army recruit. But at that moment I wished I was wrapped in it from head to toe. Maybe then it could have covered my burning face and camouflaged me enough to make me disappear in the bushes bordering the practice field.

"Tough luck, JoJo," Jimmy said. He tried to keep his face straight, but his comment ended in a loud guffaw.

"Shut up, Jimmy," I growled. My embarrassment turned to anger.

We each got two turns at the long jump. On my second try, I gritted my teeth and powered into the jump. It was good. Not as good as Jimmy's, but it was at least respectable.

But each event was like that. Jimmy constantly showed off, and when he succeeded in beating me, rubbed it in unmercifully.

I found myself hating him. I know that it's wrong to hate people, but I couldn't help it. I always knew Jimmy was brash and obnoxious, but this behaviour revealed an ugly side to him, something that couldn't be brushed off or joked about. The burping contest I'd had with Jimmy in the fifth grade was good-natured and fun, even if it was gross. This was a fight to the finish.

Mr. P. began to grow tired of Jimmy's comments, and so did Leah.

"Brader, put a cork in it, will ya?" she barked, before beginning her curving sprint to the bar in the high jump. Her long legs exploded with power, her back arched and she flew gracefully over the bar. She landed on the thick mat with a soft, sinking plop and somersaulted backwards, laughing as she crawled off.

"Okay Brader, top that," she challenged.

Jimmy clenched his jaw and I could see the concentration in his face. He rocked back and forth on his feet before he raced toward the bar. He leaped up … his back arched … I held my breath.

His shoulders hit the bar and Jimmy tumbled down to the mat on top of it. He was just too bulky to get himself over the bar. He didn't look up as he rolled off the mat.

It was the best thing that could have happened.

Leah didn't brag about her triumph, and neither did I, but it restored my confidence. Jimmy wasn't the best at everything after all, and now he knew it.

Finally the events were over, and we lined up for lemonade before the Athletic Challenge. A nervous quivering fluttered in my stomach.

This was it.

11

Me and My Twin Broomsticks

Let's get this show on the road," Leah said. Most of the grade seven students who weren't competing loitered on the field, waiting for the challenge to begin.

"Okay, everyone," Mr. P. called. "Let's do the 100-metre sprint first. All four competitors from each team will compete at the same time."

Everyone gathered eagerly near the track to watch. The girls cheered as Leah and the girl from Nancy's team came forward.

Leah grabbed me by the elbow. "Josie," she whispered urgently. "I think I've got to go to the bathroom."

"What?" I said. "You can't go now. Go after your race."

"I can't," she moaned. "That's the problem. I'm totally scared. I've never competed with this many people watching before. What if I mess up in front of all my friends?"

I glanced at her, surprised. She was the last person I thought would be affected by nerves. Even though I often tensed up, I was used to people watching me compete.

"Listen to me," I said. "Focus on your event. Don't worry about them. If you concentrate hard enough, you'll forget everything else."

She shot me a withering stare. "Thanks. That's really helpful."

I thought about how Beth's advice had given me something specific to work on for my 200-metre butterfly, and how similar Leah was to me, in that respect. In order to improve, we both needed something definite to focus on.

"Listen," I whispered. "If you really focus on the race, you'll forget they're even there. Think about your technique. Remember to explode from the block. Remember to breathe properly. And if you're still nervous, imagine that everyone who's watching is standing in their underwear."

"What?" Leah looked shocked. "That's perverted!"

"No, it's not. It's a public speaking technique. Dale, my swimming coach, told me about it. If everyone is in their underwear but you, you have an edge. You're in control. Get it?"

"Is this another one of those hooey-balooey things?"

"Sort of."

Leah shook her head, squared her shoulders and marched to the starting line. But a small smile hovered around her mouth as I saw her glance at the crowd of kids on either side of the track.

"Take your marks." Mr. Wentworth raised his whistle. "Tweet!"

Leah shot away from the start like a bullet. She flew across the grass and sprinted for the finish line.

Her quick start wasn't enough, though. The boy from Jimmy's team wasn't terrific — it was obvious that he hadn't done much practising — but he had enough speed to pull alongside her. He edged ahead. With an extra burst of speed, Leah managed to stretch forward just at the finish line.

"TIE!" roared Mr. P. gleefully.

Jimmy eyed me gloomily, but I couldn't keep the grin off my face. I ran down the grass to congratulate Leah, and our team jumped up and down crazily for a few minutes.

It was a great start.

As the events wore on, Jane made a tolerable showing in shot put, although the boys from both teams beat her. Carmen tied with the girl from Nancy's team in the obstacle course, but they both clobbered the boys! Carmen's agility sped her through the course as though she had quicksilver in her toes. Delaney came last in hurdles. She was disappointed, but as I pointed out, she was competing against Nancy Buko, the seventh-grade track star, and both of the boys had run the hurdles at the last track meet. Delaney would've needed wings to beat those three.

Beth came second in rope climbing. The boy from Jimmy's team beat her, but she was close. Just Randi, Marion and I still had to compete.

We waited in the gym after Beth competed. The last three events would be held here, and the big room was filled with the tense silence of people waiting. The bleachers were filled, and as the eighth and ninth graders finished their sports, they stopped to see what was going on. Soon the gym was packed with clusters of kids crowding along the walls. The seventh graders held whispered discussions about the next events.

"All right, everyone," Mr. P. yelled. "The sports quiz is next."

Marion sat up very straight.

"Quiz competitors please have a seat up here." Mr. P. gestured to the row of four chairs near the front of the gym. "This will be very informal. First person with their hand up gets to answer. If they answer incorrectly, the second person gets a chance, and so on. Each correct answer will be awarded one point. Incorrect answers will have one point deducted from the total score. It's possible, then, to have a negative score, so I would not encourage guessing." He looked around at all of us. "And there is to be no prompting, facial expressions, or other gestures from the audience to assist the competitors. That is cheating, and if I catch anyone doing it, your team is automatically disqualified. Is that clear?"

Everyone nodded. The four competitors trooped up to the front of the gym. Nathan Oswitz was the boy from Jimmy's team, and he looked very nervous. In spite of a name that made me think of textbooks and glasses, Nathan was a very serious jock. Everyone called him Nat, and he was almost as brawny as Jimmy. Which might explain why he looked as though he couldn't figure out why he was going to have to use his brains in an athletic contest.

Marion looked over and gave me a calm smile. Don't worry, her look said. I have everything under control.

Mr. P. unfolded a sheet of paper and studied it for a moment. "All right. First question. Which Canadian swimmer won a gold medal for the 100-metre backstroke in the 1992 Summer Olympics?" he asked.

I knew that, of course. I chewed frantically on a thumbnail and hoped Marion had the answer.

She did. Her hand shot into the air. "Mark Tewksbury," she said.

"Correct." Mr. P. looked pleased. I slowly let my breath out. I hadn't even realized I was holding it.

"Next question. In which sport is the Stanley Cup a pinnacle award?"

Marion's hand shot into the air, followed by Nat's, but the girl from Nancy's team was first. "Hockey," she said.

"That's right." Mr. P. made a mark in his notebook.

Jimmy glared at Nat. Nat began to look flustered.

"In which sport is a 'triple axel' a key component?" asked Mr. P.

In a move born of desperation, Nat threw his hand in the air. "Uh … car racing?" he said.

"No, I'm sorry, Nat. That's incorrect."

Nat wilted.

"Marion?" Mr. P. turned to her.

"Figure skating." Marion tried not to look smug.

I was having trouble not jumping up and down with glee. I tried to suppress the silly grin that wanted to surface, and avoided the glare that Jimmy directed at me. He certainly wasn't happy.

"Who was the Canadian runner who won a gold medal for the 100-metre event in the 1996 Summer Olympics?" Mr. P. fired off.

Marion's hand was first up. "Donovan Bailey," she said.

It went on like that. Marion waxed them all. I think Nancy's team got a total of two points, the other boy's team received one, and Nat remained at minus one. I think Nat was afraid to try again, even if he had managed to get his hand up quicker than Marion. She was so fast, I began to hope that she wouldn't suffer from a dislocated shoulder.

"Okay, that's it!" Mr. P. finally clapped his question sheet back inside his notebook. "Let's move on to the next events."

There was a scraping back of chairs as the four competitors stood up and returned to their teams. Marion, flushed with triumph, sat down beside me.

"I told you those articles I found in the library would help," she whispered.

I nodded and gave her a quick thumbs-ups sign. "Great job!" I said softly.

"Okay, everyone. The sit-up competition is next, and then push-ups," Mr. P. said. He motioned to the mats laid out on the gym floor. "Competitors have one minute to do as many sit-ups and two minutes to do as many push-ups as possible."

Randi gave me a nervous glance.

"You'll be great," I whispered. I knelt down on the mat by her feet. For sit-ups, the competitors were allowed to have a partner to count and hold their feet down to make the sit-ups easier on the lower back. Ross was parked on the mat beside us, with his partner from Jimmy's team. Sit-ups were not his strong point, and I wondered how Randi would fare against him.

I knelt firmly on Randi's toes and wrapped my arms around her calves. "Ready?" I asked.

She nodded.

Mr. P. blew the whistle. Randi swung up into the first sit-up, her elbows pointed at me like arrows. "One," I said under my breath. "Two. Three. Four …" Randi's face began to look like a ripe raspberry, but she kept going, faster and faster.

The seconds ticked by. "Sixty-two, sixty-three, sixty-four," I counted. Mr. P. kept his eyes glued to the stop watch.

"And … stop!" he announced.

"Sixty-eight," I said. "Way to go, Randi! That's an all-time best."

She gave a groaning gasp and flopped back onto the mats. "Thanks." She wiped the sweat from her forehead.

Mr. P. wrote down the scores, and I was pleasantly surprised to discover that Randi had placed first.

She squealed in delight. "I won!" she crowed. "Josie, I won!"

Ross had placed second, just behind Randi with sixty-seven sit-ups. He didn't seem too upset, but I noticed the mixed expression of discomfort and frustration on Jimmy's face, and felt the beginnings of another grin twitch at the corners of my mouth.

Maybe things would work out okay, after all.

But then it was my turn and when I found out who I was competing against, my insides froze.

Jimmy.

I had no idea we'd both chosen the same event — push-ups. I could have kicked myself for not seeing this coming. Jimmy flexed his arms and gave me a shark-toothed smirk. I glanced at my own arms, which looked like twin broomsticks compared to Jimmy's heavy muscles, and felt my confidence slide away. This was just like the time I'd raced against Ross in practice a few weeks ago. I'd had no chance then, and I had no chance now.

It doesn't matter if you don't win, I told myself. The point was to come out and show Jimmy that we could compete fairly against him and the other boys. We've done that. We proved that working hard pays off.

So why did I feel so crummy about possibly losing my event to Jimmy Brader? Simple. He was a jerk, and I would have dearly loved to see him fall flat on his face.

"Everyone ready?" Mr. P. asked.

I knelt down on the mat and gritted my teeth. I was not going to give up and quit. Jimmy was not going to win without any effort, that was for sure.

"Tweet!" Mr. P. blew the whistle.

I shoved my body down toward the mat and forced my arms to propel me up with all the speed I could muster.

"One," Randi counted softly. "Two. Three. Four. Five."

"Come on, Josie! You can do it!" I heard Delaney's voice from the sidelines.

Up, down, up, down. The mat kept coming into focus, then blurring as my face rushed toward it. Beads of sweat trickled down my face. I tried to breathe evenly and ignore the hot, cramping ache in my muscles. Out of the corner of my eye, I could see Jimmy's arms pumping furiously. I looked at the mat again.

"One minute," said Mr. P.

I groaned. One minute to go.

"Come on, Josie!" Randi's voice was urgent. "Keep going. You're keeping up!"

My arms begged me to slow down, but I forced myself to go faster. My training for swimming began to pay off, because I've had lots of practise ignoring the pain and staying focused on the race. I breathed. I pushed. I watched the mat. And I kept going.

"Sixty-one. Sixty-two. Come on, Josie!" Randi hissed.

"Faster, Josie! Come on, you can do it!" Leah yelled.

Jimmy began to slow down. I could hardly see, I was so tired, but I could tell his arms weren't moving as fast. I pushed harder.

Ross began to cheer. "Come on, Josie! Way to go!"

"Seventy. Seventy-one." Randi counted louder this time.

"And ... time!" Mr. P. yelled. "Stop!"

"Seventy-three!" Randi cried.

I blinked and collapsed on my stomach on the mat. My arms felt like limp spaghetti. I could hardly even tell if they were still attached to my body.

"Are you okay, Josie?" Randi asked worriedly.

I flopped onto my back. "Yeah. I think my arms are about to fall off, though."

Mr. P. scrawled down the scores. "Well, folks. We have a tie for first. Both Jimmy and Josie had a total of seventy-three push-ups."

Jimmy scowled and kicked at the mat.

"Really?" I beamed as Leah pulled me up and thumped me on the back.

Mr. P. winked at me, and I stood still with a sudden realization. I'd wondered why Mr. P. had set a two-minute time limit to the push-ups, when sit-ups were only one, but hadn't questioned it. Now I knew why. That sneaky Mr. P.! He knew all along that Jimmy and I would be competing head-to-head, and he set it up so I would have an advantage. He knew that Jimmy had more strength, and that endurance was the only thing I had going for me. I had told Mr. P. that, after the race between Ross and me. I caught the wink he threw me and grinned.

After all, it was fair. Sneaky, but fair. I had tied with Jimmy all by myself. Just me and my twin broomsticks.

12

Showdown

The wait was killing me. Mr. P. was taking forever. The challenge teams were clustered near the front of the gym, and the spectators were milling around by the bleachers. The guys on Jimmy's team, including Ross, seemed to be having a good time, but Jimmy stood with his arms crossed and preserved a smouldering silence. I read that phrase in a book once — "preserved a smouldering silence" — and it seemed to suit Jimmy exactly. I could practically see the smoke wafting from his ears, he looked so mad. It was obvious that he felt his team hadn't lived up to his expectations.

My team was goofing around too, now that the pressure was off, but I was too nervous to join in.

"How long can it take to add up the scores?" I complained.

In answer, Mr. P. stepped back into the gym. Mr. Wentworth was with him, along with Ms. DePalma, the girls' gym teacher.

"All right folks!" Mr. P. gave us a broad smile. "We've got the results of the first ever seventh-grade Athletic Challenge!"

Everyone waited expectantly.

"I'll explain the scoring first. In all events, ten points were given to the first place team, eight to the second, six to the third, and four to the fourth. In the sports quiz, ten questions were asked, and the competitors were given one point for each correct answer. To be fair, we've taken those scores, determined the placings, and given the same amount of points as with the other events. That way, no extra weight was given to any one event. In all the events, ties were awarded equal points. For example, first place ties were given ten points each."

I was listening carefully to this explanation, but I still felt puzzled. Jimmy looked downright confused.

"In fourth place, Nancy's team, with forty-six points."

Nancy's team looked extremely disappointed.

"In third place, Phil's team, with fifty-five points."

I chewed at my already-ragged thumbnail.

"Jimmy's team was second, with a total of sixty-six points."

A loud burst of cheering drowned out Mr. P. as every girl in the gym let out a whoop of triumph.

"And in first place …" Mr. P. shouted above the noise, "Josie's team with a total of sixty-eight points!"

I felt a bubble of pride swell in my chest. We had really done it. Against all the odds. In spite of all the criticism. I felt terrific.

Jimmy stood behind me. "Aw, the scores were probably rigged," he muttered, loud enough for me to hear.

That's all it took. All the great feelings I had had vanished and anger replaced them … a white hot anger that made me shake all over. I couldn't believe that Jimmy was still as narrow-minded and obnoxious as ever. Hadn't the Athletic Challenge taught him anything?

I whirled around. I couldn't stop my hands from shaking as they gripped into fists. As I groped for the right words to tell Jimmy where he could put his bigoted attitude once and for all, Ross interrupted.

"Aw, Brader, lighten up," he said. "It's not the first time a girl's whipped your butt, and it won't be the last."

"Yeah, Jimmy." One of the guys laughed. "It's no big deal. Josie is just as good as you, so why don't you admit it?"

"He can't," someone else piped up, snickering. He thrust out his chest and sang, off-key, "He's got to be ... a macho man!"

That broke everybody up. The guys on Jimmy's team laughed so hard I thought they'd wet their pants. Even my team was giggling.

I was glad that the other boys on the teams seemed more easy-going about losing. Some of my anger eased, and I took a deep breath. I wanted to say something, but this time I considered it carefully.

Nat, the boy who had competed against Marion in the sports quiz, gave another derisive hoot. "Yeah, Brader, just wait until you get a job and *your* boss is a girl! Are you going to challenge her to see who can do more push-ups?" Nat shot Marion a smile, but Jimmy's face turned purple.

"Look, you guys, this whole idea was stupid," he exploded. "If we'd practiced more, there's no way the girls would have beaten us, even with rigged scores."

Mr. P. looked as though he was about to say something, but I broke in.

"Listen, Jimmy," I said quietly. "It's bad enough that you have these warped ideas about girls and sports, but if you want to be a jerk and a sore loser on top of it ..."

Jimmy took a step forward. "Oh, yeah, Waterson?" he said, his chin jutting out. "So what does that make me?"

"Prejudiced," I said quietly. "Isn't that enough?"

13

The Last Great Race

Josie! Wake up! You're going to be late." My mother rapped on my bedroom door and poked her head in. "Didn't you set your alarm?"

Groggily, I sat up in bed. "Set it for what?" I opened a bleary eye and groaned when I saw it was only five-thirty A.M.

Mom flicked on the light and pointed to my swim bag in exasperation. "The swim meet! It's today. Did you forget?"

I leaped out of bed in a panic. "I didn't forget. I'd never forget something like that. I just didn't remember, that's all. There was so much going on yesterday …" I tried to pull my jeans over both legs at once and nearly fell over. "Anyway, I'll be ready in a minute. What time do I have to be there?"

"Six o'clock. If you hurry, you'll have time for some breakfast. I'll go make something for you."

"Nothing heavy!" I yelled after her. "Just some toast and fruit or something."

"I know, I know." Mom's voice followed her down the stairs. "I've done this before, you know."

I tugged on a sweatshirt, stuffed some clean towels in my swim bag along with my competition swimsuits, my team T-shirt and my warm-up jacket to wear between heats, and checked to make sure I had at least two pair of goggles and a few swim caps, just in case I needed extras. My bag was stuffed to the brim, but I managed to zip it closed, ran a comb through my hair and clattered down the stairs to the kitchen.

Melissa stuck her head out of her bedroom just as I hit the bottom step. "Hey, could you keep it down? Not everyone gets up in the middle of the night, you know. Some of us are trying to sleep."

"Sorry." I dashed into the kitchen. I heard Melissa clomp back to bed.

Mom put a plate of strawberries, sliced cantaloupe, toast and some scrambled eggs in front of me.

I looked at the egg warily. "Mom, I don't think …"

"Eat it. You need the protein. I only scrambled one."

I gave up worrying about protein and dug in hungrily. "Thanks, Mom."

Finishing quickly, I dumped my plate in the sink and stuffed a few granola bars into my jacket pocket. I knew I'd be starved by the time the meet was over.

Dad, who had been waiting patiently in the car while I ate my breakfast, drove me to the sports centre instead of the pool, where my team usually practises. This year, Calgary was hosting the Provincial meet, and since swimmers were coming from Lethbridge, Edmonton, and just about every-where in Alberta, we needed a big facility. The sports centre had a fifty-metre pool, which was divided into two twenty-five metre pools for this meet. This meant that two different races could swim at the same time. There was also a big dive tank, which the swimmers could use for warming-up before a heat.

The place was already packed with swimmers. I saw warm-up jackets from at least four different Calgary swim clubs, and I couldn't even tell how many from other cities. I put on my own warm-up jacket and searched the crowd for Ross. For a minute I wondered what Nationals would be like, if Provincials seemed like such a big deal, but I squashed that thought. I didn't want to think about Nationals. I didn't want to worry about equalling my record. I just wanted to swim my best.

I gave up searching for Ross and went downstairs to get changed. The locker room was a scrambled knot of giggling girls, most of them from the swim meet. I ignored them, stowed my clothes in an empty locker, grabbed my swim bag, and hurried out on deck.

I saw Dale down at the far end of the pool, near the dive tank, along with the rest of the team. I went over, stashed my bag under one of the bleachers, and sat down. Ross plunked himself down beside me.

"So, how's it going?" he asked, as if this were just any other day.

"Okay."

"Brader really ticked me off yesterday. I was glad when you stood up to him."

"For a minute I was so mad I wanted to hit him," I said. "He can be such a total creep."

"Yeah, I know. But there will always be narrow-minded jerks like Brader. There's not much you can do except deal with it."

"I guess." I couldn't resist teasing him. "Like I had to deal with your lousy attitude a few weeks ago."

"Hey, I was a jerk, but at least I've changed."

"Maybe. The jury's still out on that."

Ross scrubbed his knuckles through my hair. I yelped and jumped away.

Ross grinned and got up. "Good luck on your race."

"Thanks." I smiled and began my warm-up. I stretched out my muscles carefully, paying close attention to my shoulders. When I felt loose and relaxed, I pulled on my cap and went over to Dale.

"Hi, Josie. The heat for 200-metre butterfly is in about half an hour. You up for it?"

"You bet," I replied, with more confidence than I felt. Even though Ross had clocked me at close to my record time, I still hadn't performed it in practice. But I could do it. I knew I could. I'd coached an unorganized team of girls to an impossible victory, hadn't I? A little thing like equalling a provincial record-breaker should be easy, right?

Hah.

I dove into the dive tank and began to swim some freestyle laps. When the nervous quivering in my stomach settled down, I switched to butterfly. Smooth, strong, long strokes, I told myself. Breathe easy, don't suck the air in gulps. And don't get all clenched up. Stay calm.

I tried. I really tried not to be nervous. I tried to remember all the great things I'd accomplished in the last few days — winning the Athletic Challenge, almost equalling my record in practice. But it didn't help much.

My hands shook as I adjusted my goggles at the edge of the pool. I'd never faced such a competition before, where so much was at stake. I knew that I could always try again to go to Nationals next year. I knew that I was only twelve years old, and that even thinking about it was a big step. But even knowing all that, I still wanted to qualify now, not next year. I wanted to prove myself. I wanted to take the next step toward becoming a top Canadian swimmer.

I took a deep breath and plunged ferociously back into the pool. I pumped my legs and arched my back and swung my arms through the stroke, hoping that the activity would help me calm down.

A hand reached down into the water and grabbed my shoulder as I turned at the edge.

"Josie, slow down!" Dale looked concerned. "You're going to blow all your energy before the race. What's the matter?"

I pulled myself out of the pool and opened my mouth to say, "Just nervous jitters," but instead I said, "Do you think it was a fluke? That *I'm* a fluke?"

"A flake, maybe, but never a fluke," Dale joked, until he saw the expression on my face. "What are you talking about, Josie?"

"Breaking the provincial record, then not being able to even touch it for months. Why can't I swim the same way all the time?"

"Because people are unpredictable, even to themselves. You can think that you've mastered a skill, and then the very next day, be unable to do it. That's one reason sports are so challenging. You have to conquer yourself again and again and again." He looked at me. "Is this helping?"

"Not really," I said.

"Josie, listen. We talked about how it was just a slump, and how if you relaxed, you'd perform better. Slumps happen to everybody. They come with the sport. And anyway, you told me how you almost equalled your time after practice last week."

"Yeah, but I'm not so sure I can do it again. When I get tense, my arm stroke goes off, and I can't seem to keep it together," I said, looking up.

Dale thought for a minute. "I've seen that. When you're frustrated, it's like you hit a brick wall. Your technique goes all to heck, you get tight and tense, the stroke gets choppy … you name it. When you relax, everything is smooth. You make it look easy. Heck, half the time I don't think you're even out of breath after those races." Dale grinned. "But I don't think you're being very fair to yourself. What you did three months ago was not just a fluke. That was Josie Waterson, swimming her best time because she's practised her butt off every day in the pool. You did it before, Josie. You can do it again."

"So you never thought about giving up on me?" I hated myself for asking the question — it seemed so weak and babyish — but I had to know the answer.

"Heck, no. You're Josie the Fish, remember?" Dale gave the top of my rubber-capped head a squeeze.

My spirits rose a little, but I still felt queasy when I thought of the race. Think about how close you came at practice the other day, I commanded myself. Dale was right, it wasn't just a fluke. I *could* do it again.

I pulled my warm-up jacket over my wet shoulders, ignoring the damp splotches my wet suit made against the fabric. I crossed my arms over my chest to keep warm. The 400-metre individual medley race was almost over. The 200-metre butterfly was next.

"You're in the first heat, Josie," Dale said. "Are you ready?"

"Yes." I stretched out my arms and the back of my legs and pulled my swim cap down lower on my forehead. I didn't want it to slip back when I dove into the pool.

I handed my jacket to Dale and slipped my goggles over my eyes before I stepped onto the starting block. My throat felt as though I'd swallowed a cork. Breathe! I thought. Breathe. Relax.

I wiggled my fingers and willed the tight feeling in my chest to leave. In spite of Dale's pep talk, I was tensing up.

"Hey, Josie! Let's move!"

"Way to go, Waterson!"

The whoops were coming from the spectators' bleachers. I peered through my now-fogged goggles to see Delaney, Leah, Carmen and everyone else from my Athletic Challenge team waving a giant multi-coloured sign that read, "Go for it, Josie!" They had drawn a happy face in one corner. My parents and Melissa were next to them, and they were cheering, too.

I couldn't help smiling. Delaney was jumping up and down, trying to make sure I saw them. I raised my hand in a thumbs-up sign. She grinned back and settled down in her seat, still holding that ridiculous sign aloft.

That dopey smile stuck to my face, and a warm glow seemed to settle in my stomach, instead of the clenched knot that had been there a moment ago. They believed I could do it. They saw me prove myself to Jimmy Brader. Now it was time to prove myself to me.

"Take your marks." The metallic voice of the announcer came over the loudspeaker.

I bent over and took a good, firm diving stance. The silence was so complete, I could almost believe I was alone in the pool.

"Beep!"

I pushed with every ounce of strength in my legs and dove. The water crashed against my ears as I hit the surface, and suddenly everything was a blur. I breathed and concentrated. Not on winning, not on Dale or my friends or my mom and dad, but on me. On every kick, every arm stroke, I tried to use my strength to work with the water, not against it. I tried to make my butterfly as smooth and effortless as Dale described.

And suddenly, it was easy. I hit the stroke perfectly. I could feel it. I was skimming through the water with the kind of speed I had dreamed about since I broke the provincial record.

I made the turns at the edge razor-sharp. On the last lap I strained for the finish and punched my hands toward the edge as I sailed in.

I heard the cheers even before I ripped my goggles off to check my time. The numbers flashed on the digital scoreboard. Lane seven — my lane — was first.

I'd really done it. Not only had I equalled my record, I'd won the race by more than four-tenths of a second. The second-place swimmer in the next lane leaned over the lane rope and congratulated me as I stared up at the clock.

All the hard work, all the worry, all the effort added up to this one moment, and inside, I sparkled.